SILLY TILLY'S THANKSGIVING DINNER

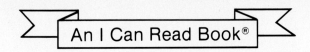

An I Can Read Book®

SILLY TILLY'S THANKSGIVING DINNER

story and pictures by

Lillian Hoban

HarperCollins*Publishers*

This book is a presentation of Newfield Publications, Inc.
Newfield Publications offers book clubs for children
from preschool through high school. For further
information write to: **Newfield Publications, Inc.,**
4343 Equity Drive, Columbus, Ohio 43228.

Published by arrangement with HarperCollins Publishers.
Newfield Publications is a federally registered trademark
of Newfield Publications, Inc. I Can Read Book is a
registered trademark of HarperCollins Publishers.

1995 edition

Silly Tilly's Thanksgiving Dinner
Copyright © 1990 by Lillian Hoban
Printed in the U.S.A. All rights reserved.
Typography by Andrew Rhodes

Library of Congress Cataloging-in-Publication Data
Hoban, Lillian.
    Silly Tilly's Thanksgiving dinner / story and pictures by Lillian Hoban.
        p.   cm. — (An I can read book)
    Summary: Forgetful Silly Tilly Mole nearly succeeds in ruining her
Thanksgiving dinner, but her animal friends come to the rescue with
tasty treats.
    ISBN 0-06-022422-3 : $ — ISBN 0-06-022423-1 (lib. bdg.) ; $
    [1. Thanksgiving Day —Fiction.   2. Moles (Animals)—Fiction.
3. Animals—Fiction] I. Title. II. Series.
PZ7.H635Sil   1990   89-29287
[E]—dc20   CIP
                                                                   AC

for
Benjamin

SILLY TILLY'S
THANKSGIVING
DINNER

It was Thanksgiving morning.

Silly Tilly Mole

was in her garden.

The leaves were falling

all around.

"Summer is gone,"

said Tilly.

"I can't remember

where it went."

9

A robin flew past.

"Good-bye, Tilly,"

he called.

"It is cold, and I am

going south."

Mr. Bunny came hopping

down the path.

He had on a scarf

and mittens.

He was pulling earmuffs

down over his ears.

"I am just practicing,"
said Mr. Bunny,
"in case we get
frost tomorrow."

"Oh dear,"

said silly Tilly.

"I forgot to remember

that winter is coming.

I forgot to remember

Thanksgiving is here."

Tilly ran
down the path
to her house.

"Wait, Mr. Bunny,"

she called.

"I have something

for you."

"What did you say, Tilly?"
yelled Mr. Bunny.
"I can't hear
with these
earmuffs on."

"I said WAIT,"

called Tilly.

She turned to look

at Mr. Bunny.

17

She ran BUMP

right into a tree.

Her glasses flew off.

18

Mr. Bunny hopped over.

"Did you say WAIT?"

he asked.

"I did," said Tilly.

"But now my glasses are gone,

and I can't remember

why I said it."

"That's all right,"

said Mr. Bunny.

"I will sit down here

and wait for you

to remember."

Mr. Bunny sat down.

TH—WUMP!

"Uh-oh," said Mr. Bunny.

"I think I found your glasses."

"Oh, thank you," said Tilly.

"That's it!" she cried.

"I just remembered

what I forgot.

It is *Thanks*giving!

I am having

Thanksgiving dinner

for all of my friends.

Wait—I will get your invitation."

Tilly put on her glasses.

She ran into the house.

But her glasses were smudged,

and everything looked foggy.

"Hmm," said Tilly.

"There is fog in my house.

I can't have fog in my house
at Thanksgiving dinner."
Tilly opened the window
to shoo the fog out.
But the fog
would not
go away.

"Tilly," called Mr. Bunny.

"I am still waiting

for my invitation."

"Oh dear," said Tilly.

"I forgot to remember

where I put the invitations,

and it is so foggy,

I cannot see

where they are.

I will get a broom

and sweep the fog out."

Tilly ran to the kitchen

to get a broom.

But she could not see.

She bumped

into the stove.

"Just in time to cook
Thanksgiving dinner,"
said Tilly.
She ran to the cupboard
to get pots and pans.

But she forgot

where she was going.

She went to the table

and got some cards instead.

"Here are the invitations,"

she said.

"Mr. Bunny," she called.

"Here is your invitation."

Mr. Bunny hopped up

to the door.

"Are they all for me?"

he asked.

"Oh dear," said Tilly.

"I forgot.

There is one for Mrs. Squirrel,

and one for Mr. Woodchuck,

and one for Mr. Chipmunk,

and some more besides.

But I forgot to remember

to send them."

"That's all right,"

said Mr. Bunny.

"I will give them out

on my way home."

Mr. Bunny looked at the cards.

The first card said,

The next card was

the recipe for

MR. WOODCHUCK'S

PINE NUT CAKE

The next card was

the recipe for

MR. CHIPMUNK'S

CRANBERRY STEW

The next card was

the recipe for

MRS. FIELDMOUSE'S

OAT BRAN

PUDDING

The last card was

the recipe for

MR. BUNNY'S

SWEET POTATO PIE

"Yum, yum," said Mr. Bunny.

"What a great idea.

This is going to be

the best Thanksgiving dinner!"

Mr. Bunny hopped off

to give out the cards.

Tilly hurried into the kitchen

to start cooking.

"Now where are

all those recipes?"

she asked.

She hurried over to her desk.

But she could not see,

and she forgot

what she was

looking for.

"Oh dear," she said.
"It is getting late
and I am tired.
I will sit near the fire
and try to remember
what I forgot."

Tilly sat down

near the fire.

She fell asleep.

When she woke up,

it was dark.

"Almost time

for Thanksgiving dinner,"

she said.

"Almost time

for my guests to arrive."

Tilly got up

to set the table.

"Oh dear!" she cried.

"I just remembered

what I forgot!

It is so foggy,

I could not see

to find the recipes.

I never cooked

Thanksgiving dinner!"

Tilly started
to sniffle.
Her eyes filled
with tears.

Just then

the door flew open.

"Who is there?"

called Tilly.

She wiped her eyes.

Then she wiped her glasses.

The fog was gone
and she could see!

She saw Mrs. Squirrel

carrying a bowl

of acorn jam.

She saw Mr. Woodchuck

with a pine nut cake.

She saw Mr. Chipmunk

with a pot

of cranberry stew.

She saw Mrs. Fieldmouse

with some oat bran pudding.

And she saw Mr. Bunny

carrying a sweet potato pie!

"Oh, how lovely!"
cried Tilly.
"Now we can have
Thanksgiving dinner!"

But just as they

sat down to eat,

they heard:

GOBBLE! GOBBLE!

GOBBLE!

The front door flew open.

In came Mr. Turkey

with a bag of corn.

"Tilly Mole,"
said Mr. Turkey,
"don't you know
you can't have Thanksgiving
without Mr. Turkey?"

"Oh, Mr. Turkey,"
said Tilly,
"*everybody* knows that!
I just forgot to remember
to give Mr. Bunny
your invitation."

So they all had

Thanksgiving dinner.

Then they sat

around the fire

and sang songs.

Mr. Turkey

made his recipe for

MR. TURKEY'S

BEST EVER

POPCORN.

And everybody said it was

the best Thanksgiving ever.